S0-BZY-404

Peter Spier's
RAIN

↑
Spi
Summer reading

To Nancy and Bob Banker: May your skies be clear and
your days be filled with sunshine!

Other books by Peter Spier

The Fox Went Out on a Chilly Night
London Bridge Is Falling Down!
To Market! To Market!
The Erie Canal
Gobble, Growl, Grunt
Crash! Bang! Boom!
Fast-Slow, High-Low
The Star-Spangled Banner
Tin-Lizzie
Noah's Ark
Oh, Were They Ever Happy!
Bored—Nothing to Do!
The Legend of New Amsterdam
People
Peter Spier's Christmas
The Book of Jonah
Dreams
Peter Spier's Birthday Cake
We the People
Peter Spier's Advent Calendar

Published by Bantam Doubleday Dell Books for Young Readers
a division of Bantam Doubleday Dell Publishing Group, Inc., 1540 Broadway, New York, New York 10036

If you purchased this book without a cover you should be aware that this book is stolen property. It was reported as "unsold and destroyed" to the publisher and neither the author nor the publisher has received any payment for this "stripped book."

Illustrations copyright © 1982 by Peter Spier
All rights reserved. For information address Doubleday Books for Young Readers, New York, New York 10036.
The trademarks Yearling® and Dell® are registered in the U.S. Patent and Trademark Office and in other countries.

ISBN: 0-440-41347-8
Reprinted by arrangement with Doubleday Books for Young Readers
Printed in The United States of America
April 1997   10 9 8 7 6 5 4 3

Peter Spier's
RAIN

A Picture Yearling Book